A *Winter's* NIGHT

Illustrated by Alison Edgson

STRIPES PUBLISHING
An imprint of Magi Publications
1 The Coda Centre, 189 Munster Road, London SW6 6AW

A paperback original
First published in Great Britain in 2010

ISBN: 978-1-84715-144-5

2 4 6 8 10 9 7 5 3

A Winter's NIGHT

Stripes

CONTENTS

THE NIGHT WATCH

Michael Broad

My name is Harry, and I'm a puppy with a mystery to solve.

I should start by telling you that my family is made up of two big people called Mum and Dad, and two small people called Holly and Jacob. When I first arrived, they taught me how to chase balls and to wee outside and to offer my paw for treats. My new family were very pleased with how quickly I learned everything, but lately they have been acting strangely and I am determined to find out why.

It all started when it snowed during the night, which made Holly and Jacob shriek as they ran downstairs the following morning. I hurried to their rescue to find them dashing around the garden throwing snowballs at each other. Snow is like rain, but colder and fluffier, and snowballs are fun to catch and eat. But the children suddenly stopped the game to build a man out of snow, giving him a carrot nose and pebbles for eyes, which was odd.

A few days later, Dad brought a tree into the living room. I had only ever seen trees outside before, mostly in the woods where my family take me for long walks. But when

I tried to have a wee against the indoor tree,
like I do with the trees in the woods, Mum
hurried me outside into the garden.

Later on, the whole family decorated the
indoor tree with twinkling lights and shiny,
brightly-coloured balls. But when I chased
the balls and tried to chew them, Holly
told me that these balls were just for
looking at and fetched my
old one to play with.
Unfortunately,
my old ball is
not very good
any more because
I've chewed it
to bits.

The next strange thing involved my favourite thing of all. Food!

I was snoozing in my basket while my family were out shopping, and when they returned, Mum staggered into the kitchen with a giant turkey and needed Dad's help to get it into the fridge. Afterwards, they filled the cupboards with more delicious food than I'd ever seen and left snacks around the house that they kept forgetting to eat. There were nuts in bowls and chocolates in tins, and after Holly and Jacob each hung a red sock on the mantelpiece – that were much too high for me to chew – they put a mince pie and a turnip on a plate above the fireplace!

I didn't care for the turnip, but the mince

pie smelled very nice, so I sat looking up at it and held out my paw, as I usually do when I see something good to eat. But instead of giving me the pie, Holly gave me a doggy treat and Jacob gave me a pat on the head, then they both hurried off to bed much earlier than usual.

No one ate the mince pie, because I kept an eye on it until Mum and Dad went to bed, too. And as they tucked me into my basket and said goodnight, I was given an unusual command.

"Don't bark at Santa, Harry," said Dad.

I love my family very much, but as I returned to the fireplace to continue gazing at the delicious mince pie, I knew something very strange was going on and I was determined to get to the bottom of the mystery.

I decided that it must have something to do with the person they called Santa. Holly and Jacob had mentioned him a few times and were very excited about his visit, and after Dad told me not to bark at Santa, I worked out that he must be arriving soon. So I waited by the front door, listening out for footsteps on the path, but no one came near the house and after a while I dozed off.

At this point you might be thinking that things couldn't get any stranger, but in the middle of the night I was woken up by the sound of hooves trotting along the roof!

My doggy instincts told me to bark and warn my family that there was livestock wandering around on top of the house, but as they had all gone to bed so early, I thought they must be very tired. So I decided to investigate the disturbance myself before raising the alarm.

Tilting my head and pricking up my ears, I soon heard a person stomping across the roof and clambering down the chimney. I quickly bounded over to the fireplace, sneezing as a cloud of soot tickled my nose, and

when I looked

up there was

a pair of

black boots

standing

on the logs!

Dogs know all about burglars, and when a man in red clambered out of the fireplace carrying a big brown sack, I forgot all about Santa because I was certain this other man had come to rob the house.

"Ho! Ho! Ho!" The burglar laughed, crouching down to pet me.

"GRRR!" I growled, and pounced on him.

Being a puppy, I am not very big, but I am quick and can leap quite high. So I leaped on the burglar's big, round belly and managed to grab his bushy white beard. He chuckled as I dangled from his beard, and when he tickled my belly, I couldn't help letting go.

By the time I was back on my paws, he was creeping towards the indoor tree. The tree didn't matter much to me because I was not allowed to use it for its proper purpose, but my family seemed to like it, so I sprang into action to protect it. I bounded across the room and grabbed the heel of his shiny black boot, and this time I refused to let go. But the clever burglar simply slipped his foot out. He tiptoed over to the tree wearing one boot and a stripy sock. I was about to go for his ankle when he did something odd.

Instead of taking things from the tree, the man opened his sack, pulled out several colourful parcels and placed them under the branches. This was my first encounter with a real life burglar, but I was pretty sure they were meant to take things away instead of bringing them, so I halted my attack while I tried to figure him out.

It was only when the man in red crept over to the fireplace to fill the socks on the mantelpiece with sweets, that I suddenly realized I had seen him somewhere before!

Around the room there were lots of cards with pictures on that the postman had been pushing through the letter box every morning. I hadn't taken much notice of them before because the first one that came didn't taste very nice and I got told off for chewing it. Now, when I looked closer, I noticed that while some had pictures of indoor trees and others had pictures of snowmen with carrot noses, most of them had pictures of the mysterious man in red!

This must be Santa! I thought, remembering what Dad had said.

I suddenly felt very bad for swinging from Santa's beard and stealing his boot and planning to bite his ankle, so I grabbed the boot and hurried over to him, wagging my tail so he would know I was friendly.

"Ho! Ho! Ho!" said Santa, slipping his foot back into the boot.

"YAP!" I went quietly, so I wouldn't wake my family.

As Santa turned back towards the chimney, he spotted the mince pie and the turnip on the plate. He slipped the turnip into his pocket and took a small bite from the mince pie. Then he looked back at me and gave a hearty chuckle.

I didn't know what Santa was chuckling at, until he stooped down and shook my paw. I'd offered it without even thinking because that's what I always do when food is around. But Santa was happy to share the mince pie. He gave me the rest of it and patted me on the head.

"Merry Christmas, Harry," he said, and climbed back up the chimney.

I bounded over to the window and caught a glimpse of Santa's sleigh as it soared through the sky pulled by seven reindeer – which explained the hooves on the roof and the turnip. Then I thought about what he had said and realized that as well as knowing *my* name, Santa had given my mystery a name, too.

It was called *Christmas*!

I was so tired after working everything out that I fell asleep with my nose still pressed against the window, and I didn't wake up until Holly and Jacob charged into the living room early in the morning.

The children gasped with joy at the

parcels under the tree, and when they unwrapped their gifts they were delighted with the toys and games and sweets that Santa had brought for them. I was equally happy chasing scraps of colourful wrapping paper around the room, but then Holly called me over.

I thought she might tell me off for chewing the paper and making such a mess, but instead she took one last parcel from under the tree and placed it in front of me.

"Santa left this one for you, Harry!" Holly said.

I held the parcel down with my paws and ripped the paper with my teeth to find the thing I wanted most in the whole world. A brand new ball to chase and chew!

Christmas is brilliant – especially for a puppy!

Later on, Mum managed to wrestle that giant turkey into the oven and there were so many leftovers I didn't even have to offer my paw. Holly and Jacob took me out into the snow to play with my new ball, and in the evening, by the light of the indoor tree, I heard Dad saying that Christmas happens every year!

I'm already looking forward to next year when my family start acting strangely again, because next time I'll know what's happening. I'll be sure to give Santa lots of wagging tail and wet licks, which will be my own special way of saying, "Merry Christmas, Santa!"

MOUSE
MAGIC

Julia Green

Molly held Granny's hand tight. Together they watched Dad drive off down the road and disappear round the corner. Molly's lip wobbled a bit. Usually she loved going to Granny's house, especially so close to Christmas. But today was different. Her baby brother Charlie was having an operation, and Mum and Dad needed to stay at the hospital with him.

"It's only for one day and one night,"

Granny told Molly. "We have lots of things to do. The time will fly by!"

Molly shivered. It was a grey, cold day. The wind made the trees sway. It began to rain.

Inside, Granny's house was warm and cosy. Granny made herself a cup of tea and heated up milk for Molly's chocolate drink. They sat down together at the kitchen table. "I've made us a Christmas *Things-to-do* list," Granny said.

Molly looked at the list. It read:

Things to do.

Bake gingerbread house

Decorate tree

Hang up Christmas stockings

"What shall we do first?" Granny asked.

"Number one, of course!" Molly said. "The gingerbread house."

Granny took down her big recipe book from the shelf and found the right page. Molly ran around the kitchen opening cupboards to get everything they needed.

Molly weighed the flour into a bowl and added the butter. She mixed them together. Next she added the sugar and two teaspoons of ginger. The spicy smell made her nose tickle. She added some milk and an egg, and stirred everything round to make a soft dough.

"Now for the best bit!" Granny said. She helped Molly to roll out the dough to make it flat. Next they put the paper shapes for the gingerbread house on to the dough and cut round them carefully, to make all the pieces for the house. There were four walls, two big pieces for the roof, and two smaller ones to make the ends of the roof. There were four little pieces to make a chimney.

While the gingerbread cooked in the oven, Molly looked at the picture in Granny's book. "How do we stick all the pieces together?" she asked.

"With sticky white icing!" Granny said. "And we use the rest of the icing to draw windows and a door, and to make a lacy pattern like roof tiles covered in snow!"

Granny cleared the table and washed up the bowls and spoons. There was a small bit of dough left over.

"Can I make something with it?" Molly asked.

"Yes, of course!" Granny said.

Molly rolled the dough flat. Very carefully, she cut out the shape of a small gingerbread mouse. To make the tail, Molly rolled out a long, thin worm of dough and stuck it on.

"What a lovely mouse!" Granny said.

"It's a present for baby Charlie," Molly said. "It's a magic mouse to keep him safe and make him better."

Granny put the gingerbread mouse on a tray in the oven to cook. The kitchen filled up with the warm, gingery smell of Christmas baking.

When the gingerbread shapes were cooked, Granny put them on a special wire tray to cool down. It took ages! At last it was time to mix the icing and stick all the shapes together to make the house.

Molly helped draw the icing door and windows. Granny did the pattern on the roof. Finally, Molly stuck on tiny sweets to decorate the gingerbread house.

"It looks magical!" Granny said. "Well done, Molly." Very carefully, Granny carried the gingerbread house over to the wide shelf on the kitchen cupboard.

Molly looked at her gingerbread mouse. He needed eyes and a nose. She picked out three tiny black sweets and stuck them on. There! Now the gingerbread mouse looked almost alive.

She placed him carefully on a plate and took him upstairs to her bedroom to keep him safe for Charlie. She put the mouse on her bedside table and went back downstairs.

Molly was so busy she almost forgot about missing Mum and Dad and baby Charlie for a little while.

After lunch, Molly and Granny went into the sitting room. In the middle of the room was a real Christmas tree in a pot. Molly sniffed the branches. She loved that pine smell! Next to the tree was a big cardboard box. Molly lifted up the flaps and peered inside. She pulled out the top layers of tissue paper. Underneath, silver baubles gleamed in the light.

"Would you like to decorate the tree, while I have a little rest on the sofa?" Granny asked.

"Yes, please!" Molly said.

First she hung the silver baubles on the higher branches of the tree. She pulled out more things from the box and hung them on the branches lower down: five wooden angels playing musical instruments like harps and drums and a flute; a robin; two white doves made of soft fabric and real feathers, and a bell that made a tiny ringing sound when she touched it.

Molly looked in the box again. Where was her favourite decoration? She fished out a small package wrapped in pink tissue and undid it very carefully. She took a deep breath. Yes! Here it was: a tiny silver trumpet made from real glass that long ago had belonged to Granny's mother, Molly's *great*-grandmother! The trumpet was very old and fragile. Carefully, Molly slipped the silver string over a branch and watched the glass trumpet slowly spin.

She found one last decoration in the box

that she hadn't seen before. It was a tiny baby lying in a walnut shell cradle. Molly thought about baby Charlie, lying sick in the hospital. She held the tiny cradle on her hand and made it rock. "Get well soon, baby Charlie," she whispered. She hung the cradle on the tree next to the silver trumpet.

Granny woke up. She looked at the tree and smiled. "Oh, Molly!" she said. "Doesn't it look magical?"

"We need something for the top," Molly said. "Can I make a star?"

"Of course," Granny answered. She fetched some felt-tip pens and card and scissors from the cupboard. She found some gold and silver glitter pens, and put them on the table next to Molly.

Molly drew a star and cut it out. She coloured it in with the pens: red, yellow, green, blue and purple, like a rainbow. She decorated the edges with glitter. Granny helped her make a hole in the top and thread some shiny gold cotton through, to make a loop so Molly could hang it from the top of the Christmas tree. It was too high up, so Granny helped Molly stand on a stool so she could reach. "Make a wish," Granny said. "You can make a wish on a star."

Molly closed her eyes and wished. *Get well soon, baby Charlie.*

"Now what?" Molly said.

"A cup of tea and a slice of cake," Granny said, "before we go and find the Christmas stockings."

Granny had made the special Christmas stockings out of soft fabric called *felt*. There was a bright pink one for Granny; a blue one for Dad; a turquoise one for Mum, and a purple one for Molly. Granny had sewed their names on the stockings with silver thread. Every year, they hung the stockings above the fireplace for Father Christmas to fill with presents.

Molly climbed the steep stairs to the attic. She liked coming up here to poke around in Granny's old things. There were pictures and books; clothes for dressing up, and even some toys that had belonged to Dad when he was a boy. Everything smelled musty and delicious. Molly found the stockings and took them back down the stairs to Granny. They hung them up above the fireplace.

"There's only four!" Molly said. "What about Charlie?"

Granny smiled. "That's our next job. We'll make a stocking for baby Charlie, for his very first Christmas. You can choose a colour for him."

Molly looked at the pieces of felt in Granny's sewing basket. The colours looked beautiful together. It was hard to choose. She picked out a soft mossy green piece. "This one," Molly said.

Granny helped Molly to fold the felt in half and draw a stocking in pencil on the back. They cut out two pieces exactly the same shape. Granny showed Molly how to sew them together all round the edges with a special stitch called blanket stitch. It took a very long time. Molly's hand ached from holding the needle and thread.

"It isn't as neat as your stitching," Molly said.

"Charlie won't mind," said Granny.

"And I haven't sewed on his name, yet!" Molly added. She yawned.

"I can do that later," Granny said.

"Now what?" asked Molly. She yawned again.

"Supper, bath and bedtime," Granny said.

"I'm going to take Charlie's stocking up to my bedroom, to keep it safe," Molly said.

Upstairs, Granny tucked Molly into bed and read her a story.

"Night night!" Granny said, closing the book. "Sleep tight, Molly. Sweet dreams." She kissed her goodnight.

"Please leave the door open so I can see the light from the landing," Molly said.

She listened as Granny padded downstairs. The house went still and quiet. Molly thought about Mum, Dad and baby Charlie at the hospital. They seemed a long way away. Molly picked up the green felt stocking she'd made for Charlie and held it against her face. "Night night, Charlie," she whispered.

Molly looked at the gingerbread mouse on her bedside table. His eyes twinkled back at her. For a second, she thought he twitched his long gingerbread tail. "Night night, magic mouse!" Molly whispered. She yawned again. She was sooooo sleepy...

Molly blinked. The gingerbread mouse was sitting up, washing his whiskers and ears with his pink paws. He twitched his nose and flicked his tail, then scurried down from the table, across Molly's pillow and over the bed. His soft, gingery fur tickled Molly's arm.

Molly watched Mouse. He seemed to be looking for something.

Mouse jumped down from the bed on to the floor. His claws made tiny scratchy sounds on the wooden boards. He scurried about. He went out of the door. When he came back, he was carrying a long piece of thread in his mouth.

He sat down in the middle of the rug. Molly kept very still so he wouldn't know she was watching him in the strip of light from the landing.

Mouse held a sewing needle in one little paw and pulled the silver thread through the eye of the needle with his teeth. Then he began to sew tiny, neat silver stitches across the green felt stocking. He was sewing letters. First a C, then an h – to make the name C-h-a-r-l-i-e.

When he had finished, Mouse tied a little knot and broke off the thread. He tugged the stocking back up on  to the bed. Molly shut her eyes tight. When she opened them again, the stocking was back on the bedside table, and so was the gingerbread mouse.

Mouse magic! thought Molly sleepily. *Now I know Charlie's going to be all right.*

It was early morning. Molly woke up. The sun was shining. The telephone was ringing downstairs. Molly listened to Granny's voice talking to someone. "Good!" Granny said. "That's wonderful news! I'll tell Molly."

Molly shot out of bed and ran downstairs. "Tell me what?" she asked.

"Your dad phoned. Everything's fine. Charlie's operation went well and he's wide awake this morning. Isn't that wonderful?" Granny hugged Molly close.

"Yes!" Molly said. "Can Charlie come home today?"

"Not today," Granny said. "He needs to stay in hospital for a little while longer. But he'll be back in time for Christmas Day. We can go and see him later."

"Can I take his gingerbread mouse to show him?" Molly said.

"Yes, if you like!" Granny said.

Molly remembered something. "Wait!" she called to Granny, as she ran upstairs.

Yes! There was the moss green stocking with Molly's silver blanket stitch all round the edges. And there, across the top in the tiniest, neatest silver mouse stitches, was Charlie's name.

Molly carried the stocking downstairs. "Look," she said. "See what the gingerbread mouse did in the night!"

"Amazing!" said Granny, although she didn't look a bit surprised.

"Like magic!" Molly said. "I told you he was a magic mouse."

Granny smiled. "I always think that Christmas is a magical time," she said. "And the best magic of all is that baby Charlie is going to be well."

"Yes," said Molly. In the sitting room, the decorations gleamed and sparkled in the light. The stockings hung over the fire.

Now everything was ready. And baby Charlie would be with them for his very first Christmas.

THE HEDGEHOG WHO WOULDN'T HIBERNATE

Guy Bass

Talltale Wood was in the grip of winter. And not the sort of winter where people say things like, "Better put a hat on, it's a bit nippy outside" – no, this was *much* worse than that. In fact, it was the coldest, harshest, most snowstormy winter since people first decided to keep a record of how cold, harsh and snowstormy winters could be. Even the forest creatures that normally thrive in winter, like the fur-backed frog and snow chicken, were huddled under rocks or sheltering in caves.

High in the treetops, a purple-breasted robin poked her head over the top of her nest.

"Yep ... it's still *freezing*," she sighed, her beak immediately frosting over. "I don't know why I feel the need to check every day – my feathers have started to grow icicles."

The robin glanced down at the snow-covered forest floor and something caught her eye. At first she thought it was a pine cone, but then she rubbed her eyes with a frosty wing and looked again.

It was a red-snouted hedgehog. The tiny creature was braving the pitiless winter, trudging bravely through the wind and snow. He bowed his head low against the driving storm, shivering from the tips of his spines to the end of his tail. The hedgehog walked on two legs (as storybook hedgehogs so often do) and carried a small bag slung over his shoulder.

"Hedgehog! Hey, hedgehog!" cried the robin. "What are you doing? You'll catch your death of cold out there!"

The hedgehog didn't hear her – or chose not to answer. He just continued to trudge his way through the snow, brushing the flakes from his eyes with a paw.

"What is he doing? Is he lost? Or maybe he got his seasons confused. Still, it's so cold even a rock must know it's winter … no one should be out in this storm. What can be so important?" mused the robin. After a moment, her curiosity got too much for her — she shook the icicles from her wings and swooped out of her nest.

"Hedgehog! Didn't you hear me? It's winter! Win-ter!" sang the robin at the top of her voice. "Shouldn't you be hibernating?"

Still, the hedgehog did not answer. He scrambled clumsily over a log and curled into a prickly ball before rolling into a snowdrift. The robin watched in amazement as he then uncurled and dug himself out. Within moments, he was on the move once more.

"Hedgehog! Where are you going? I have to know!" she said.

The hedgehog stopped in his tracks. Without looking up, he replied, "Follow me, and you'll see."

With that, he continued on his way. So, against her better judgement, the robin followed.

After several hours of following the determined little hedgehog through the snowstorm, the robin was cold and tired. She had flown after him as he tramped across snow-blanketed meadows, over logs, rocks and even a huge fallen tree, all the time fighting against the icy winds.

"Hedgehog! You said I should follow you to find out where you're going, but so far all I've got is a probable case of *robinfluenza!*" said the robin. "I demand to know what is so important that you'd risk being out here in this storm, when you should be hidden away in a nice, warm nest!"

The hedgehog stopped at the banks of a wide, frozen river.

"Follow me, and you'll see," he repeated.

"Hedgehog, wait!" cried the robin. "Don't you see, at the other side of the river? A fox!"

The hedgehog peered through the snow to the distant riverbank. There, a lesser-spotted fox had already caught sight of him. The half-starved creature was already licking his lips in anticipation of a snack (even one covered in spines). The hedgehog took a deep breath and stepped cautiously on to the ice.

"Hedgehog! Don't do it! Even if you make it across the river, that fox will gratefully eat you up!" cried the robin, but the hedgehog ignored her warning. He made his way carefully across the ice, edging closer and closer to the now drooling fox.

"Am I seeing things?" muttered the fox to himself. "It seems like that hedgehog is coming right towards me! Since when  did my dinner start being delivered? My day is looking up…"

"Fox! Hey, Fox!" cried the robin, swooping high over the fox's head to avoid being snapped out of the air. "Don't eat that hedgehog!"

"First, my mum told me never to talk to robins – she said you're all too chirpy for your own good," replied the fox. "And second, of course I'm going to eat that hedgehog. He's coming right towards me – practically walking into my open jaws. He clearly *wants* to be eaten. Who am I to deny a stupid forest creature his dying wish?"

"Look, I know this is going to sound weird, but if you eat that hedgehog now, my whole day will have been wasted," said the robin. "I've been following him to try to find out where he's going and why he's refusing to hibernate. I beg you, wait a little longer to crunch him between your jaws."

"Hang on, you mean he's been wandering through this storm?" asked the befuddled fox. "But these winds could flay the fur from a winter wolf! Why would a humble hedgehog risk everything and go out in this wild weather?"

"Exactly," said the robin. "And if you eat him we'll never find out."

"Hedgehog! Tell me where you're going and I promise not to eat you … for a couple of hours, anyway," said the fox, as the hedgehog dragged himself up the bank of the river. "Hey! I said where are you going? I have to know!"

"Follow me, and you'll see," replied the exhausted hedgehog.

With that, he continued on his way. So, against his better judgement, the fox followed.

Before long, dusk had started to drag its grey blanket across the sky. The robin and the fox followed the little hedgehog through forests, up hills and across frozen rivers. Still, the hedgehog did not stop.

"So where do *you* think he's going?" whispered the fox, as they made their way through a deep, icy valley.

"It has to be somewhere important,"

replied the robin, fluttering overhead. "Perhaps he's taking an offering to the forest gods, so that they'll free us from this horrible winter."

"Or maybe he's a human prince, cursed to wear the *shape* of a hedgehog," said the fox. "Maybe he's searching for a magical cure – a way to turn himself back into a person!"

The robin and fox continued to debate what could possibly be important enough for the hedgehog to journey through the frozen forest, but as night fell they became so cold and tired that they no longer had the strength to speak. They soon had trouble keeping up with the tiny hedgehog, who stopped only in the face of the strongest wind, curling into a ball until it was safe to continue. After a few hours, the robin and fox were convinced another minute in the punishing cold of the snowstorm would mean the end of them.

"J-Joke's over, Hedgehog!" said the fox. "We're too c-cold to follow you any more! Tell us where you're going, or I'll eat you, spines and all!"

"Follow me, and you'll see," said the hedgehog.

"You've been saying that *all day*," snarled the fox, "but we haven't seen anything but this frozen forest for hours!"

"The fox is right," said the robin. "I'm sorry, Hedgehog, but unless you tell us where you're going, I'm going to let the fox have you as a snack…"

"There," replied the hedgehog, pointing. In the distance, the animals could see an orange glow coming from a hollow in the base of a nearby tree. Suddenly, the hedgehog starting running as fast as his tiny legs could carry him. The robin and fox wasted no time in chasing after him. Their minds raced with possibilities as they watched the hedgehog scurry inside the hollow. They cautiously peered inside.

By the warm glow of a small fire, they could see a dozen more hedgehogs. The little creatures greeted their visitor with laughter and welcoming hugs. In the middle of the hollow was a feast of hedgehog favourites — roast caterpillar (with all the trimmings), minced maggot pies, grub pudding, and a large snail shell filled with warm beetle juice.

In one corner sat the top of a pine tree surrounded by presents of all shapes and sizes. The little hedgehog opened his bag, took out a pawful of tightly-wrapped presents and placed them under the tree.

"Christmas..." said the robin. "I forgot all about it."

"Wait, that hedgehog risked his spines for Christmas? He travelled day and night through the unforgiving forest, through the snow and wind, across fallen trees and frozen rivers and very nearly into my belly for *Christmas?*" asked the baffled fox. "Why?"

"Follow me, and you'll see," said the hedgehog with a smile, and beckoned them inside.

The robin was too cold to argue and hopped into the hollow. After a moment, the fox gave a shrug and followed. To their surprise, both creatures were welcomed with cheers and invited to join the hedgehogs' banquet. Before long, the hedgehogs and their guests were happily crunching and munching their way through the insect feast (even the fox, who decided it would be bad form to eat such generous hosts). The hedgehogs laughed and joked. The robin and fox joined in, entertaining the gathered hedgehogs with tales of their journey.

Soon, with full bellies and warm, dry fur and feathers, the robin and fox felt better than they had in months. For the rest of the night, the little hedgehog and his friends exchanged presents, played games and told bad jokes until they laughed themselves hoarse. The robin and fox couldn't have been happier that they'd followed the little hedgehog. The trials of winter seemed smaller than snowflakes, as their laughter and the crackling fire drowned out the whistling winter wind.

THE NIGHT
OF THE
SNOWRIDERS

Elizabeth Baguley

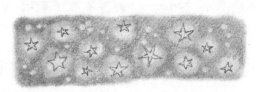

"Look!" said Noah. The other boys followed Noah's pointing finger across the flat land and dark ditches of the fen. The cold air was glittering with specks of floating ice, fiery in the setting sun.

"Angels'-breath snow," said Ezekiel, Noah's older brother. "It's what we've been waiting for – the final sign."

They had already seen the other signs: a sky so clear that you could see almost up to heaven and a wind from the east, sharp as broken glass. Now, when all the signs came together on Midwinter's Eve – the longest and most magical night of all the year – the boys would have the chance of a lifetime. For tonight the Snowriders would come.

"When darkness falls we'll race to meet the Snowriders, and the boy of greatest heart will ride the snowstorm with them," said Ezekiel.

"But what does that mean, Zeke – *the boy of greatest heart?*" asked Noah, puzzled. Grandfather had often told him the legend of the Snowriders. Once in a lifetime, they would ride through the night sky on their huge horses, drawing behind them the blizzard of blizzards. But when Noah had asked Grandad what "greatest heart" meant, he'd simply answered, "When the time comes, you'll know."

"It certainly doesn't mean you," said Ezekiel. "It will be the strongest, the fastest, the bravest boy – the one who meets the storm first. Now," he commanded the others, "go and fetch your horses!" and he strode towards the farm on his long legs.

Zeke had reached the stable long before Noah.

"What are you doing here, *little* brother?" he asked Noah. His mouth was curved into a thin smile, but his eyes were cold.

"I'm joining the race to reach the

Snowriders," said Noah.

Zeke looked down from the saddle of Midnight, a gleaming black stallion which their father kept for hunting. "You?" he said. "You're far too young."

"It doesn't stop me being brave," said Noah, stubbornly.

"But you'll hardly be the fastest if you ride on that old donkey," Zeke sneered, aiming a kick at a small grey pony as he rode Midnight out into the darkness.

Noah rubbed the pony's muzzle. "Don't listen to Zeke," he said, quietly. "He doesn't understand how special you are."

Noah had loved the gentle pony from the moment his mother had sat him on her shaggy back. *Horse.* Her name was the first word he'd ever spoken. Now, he told her everything. She understood how unhappy he was when Zeke – their father's favourite – was given fine new clothes, while Noah had to manage with old ones which were far too small for him. She listened to his anger when Zeke was allowed to ride and shoot all day, while Noah had to get up at dawn to work on the farm. In return for her patience, Noah would never overload her cart or beat her when she was tired. He loved Horse as she loved him.

"Tonight, we'll be as good as my brother and Midnight," Noah said, leaping on to

Horse's bare back. Together they rode out into the dusk.

Out on the wind-blown fen, the other boys were already lined up, waiting. Zeke faced them.

"When the Snowriders appear, gallop as fast as you dare," he said. "Those of you on donkeys," he looked straight at Noah and Horse, "must keep out of the way so that the best of us aren't held back. Now, get ready!"

How could they have been ready for what was about to happen? From over the horizon came the echoing beat of thundering hoofs. Then a great tide of clouds swept in, swallowing the stars. The clouds were pulled by huge, white storm-horses. Riding them were winged giants – angels with pale, shining faces whose white hair and cloaks streamed behind them. The horses' white tails were lost in a great fountain of snow that sprayed out over the dark fen.

Now was the time. The race to be the fastest, bravest, strongest – to be the first to meet that fountain of snow – began. Zeke was the first to urge his horse into a gallop, but he was quickly followed by the other boys. Noah leaned forward over Horse's neck, holding on to her mane. He had never felt such excitement. The Snowriders were slowly pulling the storm over the vast, black sky and soon the leading boy – the boy of greatest heart – would be chosen to fly with the angels on the surge of the blizzard.

It was not easy. The wind pushed like invisible hands against Noah and Horse. The little pony stretched forward, strong from her long hours of working in the fields. Noah, used to Horse's every move, was like a limpet on her back. Behind them, many of the boys had already stopped, their horses tired and panting. Others had fallen off and their horses galloped on by themselves. Horse dodged the riderless animals without Noah having to guide her. "Clever lass," said Noah, then added in surprise, "We're almost at the front."

Pitcher's Dyke, a strip of black water, came suddenly into view. It looked too wide to jump, but jump it they must. Zeke and

Midnight took the stretch of icy blackness in their stride. A scream and a splash told Noah that the stretch of water had been too great for the horse and rider between him and Zeke. Surely this would be the end of Noah's dreams, too.

"Please, Horse," Noah whispered. He closed his eyes, certain that she couldn't possibly reach the other side – but somehow she did, and they landed safely.

So, now it was Noah against Zeke, Horse against Midnight.

Second, thought Noah. *I am always second.* He was the second born, second in height and, worst of all, his father's second favourite.

When, for a moment, Zeke turned and looked at Noah with his cold smile, something exploded in Noah's head. He pressed his heels into Horse's sides. Horse was determined to do her best for her master and made her stride longer. Little by little, they began to catch up with Zeke on his sleek stallion. Above and in front, the Snowriders flew towards them on magnificent wings of crystal white feathers. *Let me fly with you*, thought Noah, with an ache that filled his heart.

But he was still second. The Snowriders were almost overhead and the sound of their hooves was like thunder. Ezekiel brought his riding whip down on Midnight again and again, spurring her on, desperate to be the boy of greatest heart. He raised his face, ready to be lifted to the sky, but shocked by the heavy beating, Midnight reared and lost ground. Faithful Horse galloped on, and when Zeke saw her catching up, he cried out in anger before throwing his whip backwards towards the little pony's legs.

Horse, unable to swerve, tripped and fell.

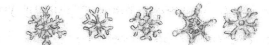

Noah's mouth was full of grit as he lay in a strange, snow-whirling silence. The Snowriders had passed overhead and their storm swept over the land. Noah moved, bruised but not broken.

Where was Horse?

She lay nearby, her eyes full of pain, her foreleg twisted underneath her. "Oh, Horse!" Noah cried. He'd wanted to be first, wanted to beat his brother, wanted to be the boy of greatest heart. How stupid he'd been. His best friend lay hurt and he didn't know how to help her. He crawled over to where she lay and cradled her head.

"I'm so sorry," he sobbed. "It's my fault you're hurt. You gave me everything you had in the race. You were strong and fast and brave, but I was selfish and thoughtless. I nearly gave your life to have a few short minutes with the Snowriders. Now I'd give everything I have to turn back time and have you better."

"No being can turn back time," said a voice. Towering over the boy and his pony was a tall, white-skinned, white-haired, white-winged rider, whose horse seemed carved from ice. "But an angel of the storm can do many things for one whose heart is so great with sadness and longing and love."

The Snowrider slid down to kneel next to Noah, then arched his wings over Horse. A starburst of light cut through the darkness, and Noah screwed up his eyes against the brilliance. When he opened them, Horse was standing, quite whole and mended. The Snowrider laid his hand on Noah's shoulder. "Someone who loves so deeply deserves to have his pony well again. You are the boy of greatest heart," he said. "Now you will ride with us."

"But I wasn't the fastest," said Noah. "My brother was first."

The Snowrider smiled. "Fastest, bravest, strongest, first − none of these means greatest of heart. Only the most loving boy can claim that title."

Then Noah found himself rising into the night air with the Snowriders. Heart-stoppingly high, but safe on Horse's back, he surged on the storm's edge with all the stars of the high heavens above. On the ground far below, a lone figure on a black stallion gaped up at Noah in amazement.

It was still night when Noah and Horse came back to the stable. Noah made Horse comfortable and then hugged her shaggy neck.

"What was it like to ride the storm, brother?" asked a voice.

Noah turned. Zeke stood behind him, the riding whip in his hands. Noah moved away, spreading his arms to protect Horse from it.

"Don't beat her," he said. "Beat me instead if you have to."

Zeke smiled a sad smile. "I think I've learned my lesson about beating," he said, breaking the whip over his knee. "If I hadn't beaten Midnight – and if I hadn't treated you so badly – I might have been the greatest of heart. Now we both know what that means. I've learned my lesson about that, too."

"Perhaps we both need to learn what it's like to be real brothers," said Noah, holding out his hand and shaking Zeke's. It was the bravest thing either of them had ever done.

Noah was nudged awake by Horse, who had found him sleeping in her straw. It was sunrise. "Perhaps I should change your name to Great-heart," he whispered to her, "now you've ridden with the Snowriders." But as she chomped the apple he had given her, he knew that he loved her just as she was. Plain Horse.

Sunbeams chased the shadows from the stable. Outside, the snow left by the Snowriders was blazing white. It was time for Noah and Horse to ride out and, as their final honour, to lead the Midwinter procession across the blazing snow of the fen – two Great-hearts, moving in time to the peal of the Midwinter bells.

THE NIGHT
FLIER

Penny Dolan

Grace was very excited. This Christmas her family wouldn't be in their flat in the city. This Christmas they would be staying in an old faraway cottage in the country.

Mum had to work for a few more days, so Grace was going to the cottage with Aunty Caroline in the morning. "I promise I'll be there for Christmas Eve," Mum told her.

"Grace can help me get everything ready," said Aunty Caroline, smiling.

Grace packed her clothes. She packed some art stuff too. She was going to make decorations so the cottage would look really lovely for Christmas.

As soon as Aunty Caroline arrived, they loaded the car with boxes and bags. Grace made very sure they didn't forget the bag of brightly wrapped presents.

Then Mum gave Grace the hugest cuddle ever. "See you on Christmas Eve, love," she said.

Grace squashed herself into the back seat, did up her safety belt, and waved back at Mum over the bundles. As they drove off, she felt a bit sad.

"Christmas Eve will soon be here, Grace," said Aunty Caroline cheerfully. Grace tried to smile, but it was hard.

At first the car edged through traffic on the city streets. After a while, the roads seemed smaller, and they drove past fields and trees. Even though the sun was shining, sheets of silvery frost lay across the grass.

Grace saw some horses standing huddled in a field. They had thick blankets on their backs to keep them warm. "Look, Aunty Caroline!" called Grace.

"Gosh! I'm glad we're snug in our car. It must be very cold out there."

"Cold enough for snow?" asked Grace.

"Perhaps," said Aunty Caroline.

Gradually, Grace began to feel sleepy, so she closed her eyes for just a moment…

Oh! She woke up as the car crunched along a gravel driveway and stopped.

Aunty Caroline stretched her arms. "That was a long journey," she said, "but we're here at last."

They got out of the car and stood for a moment in the dusk. There was no sound of traffic and no street lamps anywhere, and the tall trees swayed and whispered around them. Ahead stood an old stone cottage that looked as if it was straight from a storybook. Grace saw a chimney at each end, two square windows peeping out of the roof and a small metal bell hanging beside the front door. It all felt slightly spooky.

"Come on. Let's go inside!" Aunty Caroline said, giving her a quick hug. "Isn't this exciting?"

She opened the door and switched on the light. Suddenly, Grace saw a big comfortable room with a sofa, and cheerful pictures on the walls, and rugs thick enough to tickle their toes. The cottage didn't feel at all spooky inside. There was even a real log fire ready to be lit.

"I like it here," said Grace, as they carried in the bags and boxes.

"So do I," said Aunty Caroline, putting down the last box. "And now we'd better have supper. Only baked beans, I'm afraid, but we'll go to the market tomorrow. We'll be able to phone your mum from there too, Grace. There's no signal here."

Grace missed speaking to Mum, but she soon cheered up. She loved beans on toast, and she loved sitting there in the cottage chatting with her aunt and watching the flames dancing in the fireplace. All too soon, it was time for bed.

Grace's room was very pretty. It was high up in the roof, and there was a small square window just by her bed. Grace knelt on the duvet and pulled one curtain back. She pressed her nose against the cold glass and peeped out at the shining, silvery moon. Something white passed by – once, twice. What was it? Grace peered out, but whatever it was had gone. She shivered.

"There aren't any ghosts here, are there?" Grace asked, as Aunty Caroline came in to read her a quick bedtime story.

"No, Grace," said Aunty Caroline, smiling. "No ghosts at all." So Grace stopped worrying, and soon fell fast asleep.

The next morning, after breakfast, Aunty Caroline and Grace explored the nearby wood. They saw frosted spiders' webs and two deer that bounded quickly away. Then they found an enormous tree lying on its side. The broken branches spread out across the ground, and there was a rough gaping hole where the roots had been torn out.

"It must have blown over in last week's storms," said Aunty Caroline.

Grace climbed up on to the huge trunk and sat there. She pretended it was a dragon and she was a princess flying bravely on its back. As she clambered down, she noticed a deep hole in the trunk. Caught in the rough bark were some soft white feathers. Grace held them gently in her hand. *I wonder where they came from?* she thought, and put them carefully into her pocket.

That afternoon Aunty Caroline took her to the market. It was great fun. They munched on hot roast chestnuts, listened to carol singers and bought more delicious things to eat on Christmas Day. After they'd phoned Mum, Aunty Caroline bought Grace some warm red mittens.

"Cold enough for snow," said the woman at the stall, blowing into her cupped hands.

"Snow?" Grace looked up hopefully, but she couldn't see a single flake.

That night, Grace knelt at the window again, peering into the darkness to see if any snow was falling yet. Suddenly, the pale white thing swished past her window again, and Grace heard a strange shrieking noise. Maybe there was a ghost after all?

Grace wished that Mum was at the cottage so she could tell her about the scary thing, but Mum wasn't, was she? "Aunty Caroline!" she called anxiously.

Her aunt hurried in. "What's wrong, Grace?"

Grace felt silly and shy. "Er ... I just wanted to say goodnight again," she pretended.

Aunty Caroline tucked the duvet tightly round her. "Try and get to sleep, love. Only three days to go until Christmas, so we're going to be very busy tomorrow."

The next morning, they drove to a nearby farm. Grace stroked the soft necks of two friendly donkeys, and fed an early newborn lamb with a bottle. They bought some vegetables and some holly and chose a Christmas tree in a scarlet pot for the cottage.

In the afternoon, Grace unpacked her art stuff and made her decorations. She cut white card into stars, and decorated each point with a silver pen, and pretty sprinklings of glitter and shiny paper.

"Shall I throw these scraps into the bin?" asked Aunty Caroline.

"No, thanks." Grace slid the scraps back into her bag in case she needed them later on.

"Would you like to decorate the tree now?" asked Aunty Caroline.

"Yes!" Grace shouted happily.

So they put the fairy lights and tinsel on

the tree. They hung Grace's stars on the branches and fixed a little angel doll at the very top. Then they turned on the lights. The tree looked very beautiful and Grace's silver glittery stars sparkled like frost.

Maybe we'll have snow tonight? thought Grace.

They had had such a fun day, but when bedtime came, Grace remembered the scary flying thing. "I'm not tired," she said in an odd cross voice.

"Well, I am." Aunty Caroline laughed. Then she looked more carefully at Grace's worried face. "What's wrong, love?"

"Something flies past my window each night," Grace admitted. "It makes me feel a bit scared."

Aunty Caroline frowned for a moment. "Shall I go outside to see what's there? I don't think it will be anything to worry about. Do you want to come? You can hold my hand if you like."

Grace nodded uncertainly. "Yes."

So they tugged on their coats and Aunty Caroline took a torch from a shelf by the door. They went outside and stood watching the trees and the big night sky overhead.

"Maybe it was the stars you saw?" said Aunty Caroline. "We can see so many from here."

"No," said Grace.

"Maybe it was the moon?"

"No, it wasn't," said Grace. "It was something sort of white and it flew about.

Like a ghost." She shivered again.

Then the moment happened. Out from between the trees flew a big bird. It swooped silently over Grace's head. It flew so low that she saw its white, heart-shaped face and soft feathery chest, and pair of pale outspread wings. Then with a loud shriek the bird disappeared again, searching for its supper.

"It's an owl!" gasped Grace. She wasn't scared now!

"He looks like a barn owl, but he's not very big yet," said Aunty Caroline. "Perhaps this is his first winter away from the nest."

Grace remembered the white feathers she'd found. "I think he used to roost in that fallen tree," she told her aunt.

The owl reappeared, soaring across in front of the cottage and away again around the corner of the building. *I wish I knew where he lives now*, Grace thought.

Afterwards, as they drank hot chocolate, Aunty Caroline told Grace about barn owls. She told her how the owls' soft feathers help them fly silently, and how they had special owl ears hidden on their flat feathery faces to help them track down the smallest sounds, especially when they were out hunting.

It was almost midnight by the time Grace got to bed. She peered out through the window once more and saw her white owl still flying around in the darkness. This time when Grace lay her head down on the soft white pillow, she heard the cries of the owl and did not feel scared at all.

That night Grace had the strangest dream. Somehow she had grown small enough to sit on the owl's back, and he was flying with her through the night sky. She wasn't in the least bit cold, because the owl's soft feathers kept her warm. Below his strong outstretched wings, Grace could see the wintry woods and fields, glittering with frost. On and on they flew, swooping through the winter air.

"Don't worry," the owl seemed to be saying. "Dream, Grace, dream…"

Grace felt him make a last great swoop right around the old cottage and suddenly she saw a narrow hole in the wall.

That must be my owl's home, she thought, and leaned over a little to see. *Oh!* Grace felt herself slipping gently off the owl's back and down, down, down as light as a feather towards her very own bed.

Grace woke early on Christmas Eve. She padded quietly into Aunty Caroline's room, but as she was still snoozing, Grace went downstairs. What could she do now? She kept thinking about her dream and wishing she could tell Mum.

That was when Grace had her owl idea. She got out all her art stuff and leftover scraps. First she folded a piece of dark card. Then she cut out a white heart-shaped face and a body and stuck them down on the front. She snipped away at small pieces of white card, making paper feather after paper feather. Grace stuck those down, and now her owl really did look like an owl. She felt in her coat pocket and found the soft white owl feathers. She glued them down too, stroking the softness. Last of all, she drew two owl feet, one sharp beak, and two very round eyes. Then she decorated the dark sky.

There it was, finished! Grace's Christmas owl, flying through the night skies with a silver paper moon behind him and glittery stars drawn in the sky. "To Mum," she wrote on the card with her silver pen, "Wishing you a Very Happy Christmas. Lots of love from Grace."

"Grace, your mum will love that card!" said Aunty Caroline, coming into the room. "What a wonderful surprise!"

"I've got a surprise for you, too, Aunty Caroline," she said. "Can we go outside right now? It won't take long."

They put coats on over their nightclothes, and their hot breath rose like mist in the cold morning. Grace led her aunt around to the side of the house and pointed up at the barn owl's new home.

"Look!" Grace said. "We're living in the owl's cottage!"

"So *that's* where he roosts! How ever did you discover that?" Aunty Caroline asked, laughing, but Grace wanted to keep her dream a secret until Mum came.

By evening, everything was ready: the rooms, the decorations, the food, the puddings and pies, the presents and the lovely sparkling tree. Grace put on her coat and scarf and waited outside for Mum to arrive.

Suddenly, Grace's owl flew into the beam of light from the half-open door, and something white came fluttering down. Grace put out her hand and caught a single warm feather, just like the feathers in her dream. Just like the feathers on Mum's card.

Then Grace laughed. More white feathers were fluttering down around her, whirling thicker and thicker. She put her hand out again, but these were definitely not warm.

"Snowflakes!" Grace shouted happily, as Mum's car appeared through the gate.

"Grace!" Mum called, as she got out.

Grace ran across to greet her. The happy Christmas had begun.

FOX FIRE

Caroline Pitcher

"Why didn't the sun get up this morning?" Little Reindeer asked his mother. "It's been dark all day long."

"That's because it's winter," she answered. "We live in a northern land. The days are gloomy and night lasts for a long time."

"So tell me a story, Mum," he said. "That will make the night go faster."

He snuggled up to shelter by his mother's warm side.

"I'll tell you the story of Little Reindeer," she began. "He could run from the moment he was born. Every day he runs across the snow on his wide snowshoe hooves. In winter, when the sun doesn't bother to get up over the horizon, Little Reindeer scrapes away snow with his hoof and eats the crispy lichen that grows underneath. Sometimes he's lucky and finds a delicious red and white mushroom, too. When summer comes again, the sun will get up, and Little Reindeer will eat the sweet green grass."

"That's *my* story, isn't it!" he cried. "I'm looking forward to summer. I don't like the winter darkness."

"It won't last for ever," murmured his mum. She nuzzled the creamy fur on the top of his head. Little Reindeer's eyes were so tired from the cold. He closed them, and soon he was fast asleep.

When he woke, he remembered the story. "Mum says I could run from the moment I was born. So here I go!"

Off he ran, across the snow on his wide snowshoe hooves, all through the forest until he reached the top of the hill. He stopped and pawed back the snow with his hoof to find food.

While he chewed the crispy lichen, he gazed down the hill. There were some houses in the distance. A man in a big coat and a fur hat came out of the wood, carrying a tree. Little Reindeer stopped chewing and stared in amazement as the man carried the tree into a house and closed the door.

He gulped down his food and ran back to his mother.

"I saw a man putting a tree inside a house!" he cried. "Why?"

"Ah, yes," she said. "People do funny things, my dear. At this time of year, they take a tree into their house and decorate it all over with little coloured lights. When they switch them on, the lights shine red and yellow and green. I think the people like to see the colours in the middle of the long gloomy winter. They call it Christmas time."

"Ooh! Can I see the lights?"

"I don't know when they'll switch them on," said his mother.

"I don't want to miss them," said Little Reindeer, "so I'll keep looking."

The next evening, he ran through the forest and up to the top of the hill on his snowshoe feet. He looked down at the houses.

But there were no coloured lights shining in the windows.

I'll run back and tell Mum there are no lights yet, he thought, and set off to find her. He ran faster and faster, enjoying the thudding of his hooves on the snow.

Oh no! There was a furry white creature in his way! Little Reindeer skidded on the snow and tried to stop, but he was going too fast. So he jumped right over it.

"Look where you're going. You nearly knocked me down!" cried the creature, swishing her bushy white tail.

"Sorry! I couldn't stop in time," said Little Reindeer. "You don't show up well. You're as white as the snow all around you."

"Of course I am. How can I get safely through the winter if everyone can see me?" yipped the creature. "I'm an arctic fox. We are white, not boring brown and grey like you reindeer. Why are you galloping through the forest like that, anyway?"

"My mum says I could run from the moment I was born," said Little Reindeer. "So I'm running to tell her that I can't see the lights yet."

"Haven't you seen them before?" asked the fox.

"No," said Little Reindeer.

"Oh, the lights are wonderful," said the white fox. She looked up at him with her golden eyes.

Little Reindeer shivered. "I don't want to miss the lights. Mum says they are switched on at Christmas time."

"Switched on? At Christmas time?" The fox scowled. "I've never heard of *that*. They shine often. But they shine brighter in the long, dark winter nights, when the magic winds blow and the skies are clear. Some say you can *hear* them."

"Hear them?" said Little Reindeer. "How can you *hear* lights?"

The fox stared at him with her golden eyes. She whispered, "They are made of a magic fire that burns above the snow. Some might call it fox fire. Look!" And she swished her bushy tail across the snow so that tiny sparks flew up into the air.

"That's beautiful," cried Little Reindeer. He felt in awe of the white fox with her strange golden eyes and her bushy tail. He thought, *I'd better stay friends with her and be polite.* So he asked, "Excuse me, Madam. What is your name?"

"My name is Aurora," whispered the white fox, and swished her tail again. She then turned and ran low into the forest, leaving behind her a shimmering cloud of fiery sparks. The sparks hovered, and for a moment Little Reindeer thought he heard music. Then they settled on the white ground and vanished.

Little Reindeer gasped and ran back to his mother.

"Where have you been?" she asked.

"I went to see if they'd switched on the lights, but they haven't. I wish they would. I'm fed up of the dark. I want to see the colours in the windows."

"They will only be small lights," said his mother gently.

"I still want to see them!" he cried. "And when I do, I'll fetch you so you can watch them too."

"Thank you, dear," said his mother.

As the days passed, it became even colder. At night-time the skies were glassy-black. At least the stars shone in the blackness, and the moon made a crescent shape, like the round edge of his mum's hoof. The moon and stars made the snow glow silvery-white, but Little Reindeer was longing to see the coloured lights.

How can you have fox fire inside someone's house? he wondered. *That white fox doesn't know what she's talking about.*

Then he remembered the fox's golden eyes that made him feel so odd and her swishy tail that conjured up the sparks, and he felt glad she could not hear him doubting what she had said.

By now, she will be roaming the forests and fells far away from here, he thought.

The next day was short and gloomy.

When twilight fell he said, "I'm just going to the edge of the forest."

"Don't be long," said his mother.

"I won't. And if the coloured lights are shining in the windows I'll run back and tell you." *Maybe tonight they'll switch them on...*

He ran through the forest and stood gazing out from the hilltop. The vast sky was so clear and black, Little Reindeer felt it was waiting for something.

He looked down at the houses.

In the window of the nearest one, he saw people. They were putting things on the branches of the tree. Little Reindeer waited and waited. He got so cold standing there alone, and he was getting hungry too.

Just when he thought he couldn't wait any longer, the little lights came on – red, yellow and green. But just as quickly, a man closed the curtains, hiding the lights from him.

Little Reindeer wanted to cry with disappointment. He'd wanted to look at the lights for longer and he'd wanted to fetch his mum to see them, too.

Then he shivered as he felt a cold wind

on his neck. He lifted up his head to look at the moon – and gasped!

Across the vast sky a sea of green flowed in waves over the darkness. As the waves rose and fell they changed. The green turned to yellow, then to red and blue. The sky was alive. The waves changed shape. They were wonderful moving swirls of scarlet, green, gold and even violet, curls and spirals and scrolls. Then they were the shapes of the pine branches and the bracken and ferns in the forest.

The colours pulsed and raged like flames, as if the sky had been set on fire by brilliant sparks.

It was magical! The lights dazzled Little Reindeer so that he could not move, as if his hooves were stuck to the snow.

"Wow!" Never had he seen anything so beautiful. They were even brighter than the moon. He stared at the shimmering sky. It shone down on the snow and changed it into a glowing land of gold, holly red and emerald.

But I haven't told Mum, he thought. *Better run!*

He turned – and there she was, walking out of the forest towards him.

"Did you know *these* lights would happen, Mum?" he asked.

"Yes. On long winter nights, the light show is more splendid than ever."

"What is this light show called?" he asked.

"The Northern Lights," said his mother. "But they have many names. People also call them Aurora Borealis, because they happen when there is a special wind."

"*Aurora?*" whispered the little reindeer. "*Aurora...*"

He looked back into the forest. Out of the corner of his eye, he saw something white behind the dark pine trees. Was it that white fox, swishing her bushy tail on the snow so that a cloud of brilliant sparks gathered in the air?

Little Reindeer put his head on one side. There was that music again.

Then the sparks vanished. So did the music, and the fox.

But the splendid Northern Lights still shone and flashed all over the sky like a magical bonfire of many colours.

"Mum," he whispered. "Do people sometimes call the Northern Lights *fox fire*?"

"Yes, they do," said his mum. "How did you know, my clever Little Reindeer?"

THE STORYBOOK WAISTCOAT

Karen Wallace

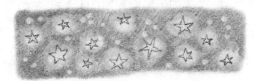

Beyond the nursery curtains, a full moon hung in the night sky like a giant pearl. Around it, millions of stars twinkled like diamonds, and the deep snow that lay on the ground glittered as if it was covered in diamonds, too.

A fire burned in the nursery hearth and a Christmas tree stood in the corner of the room, decorated with red and green balls and a gold star on the top.

In her corner beside the bookshelf, Emily the Elephant opened her eyes and climbed slowly to her feet. She was made out of soft grey felt and her tusks were knitted with white wool. Emily stretched out her long trunk and shook herself awake.

It was Christmas Eve and Emily had a special job to do.

A clockwork bell with a bright blue rope hung from the bottom branch of the Christmas tree. Emily pulled the rope with her trunk, and the next second a Christmas carol filled the room.

Oh, Jingle Bells! Jingle Bells! Jingle all the way!

Oh, what fun it is to ride in a one horse open sleigh!

Charlie Rat sat up with a start and rubbed his eyes. He was made of black corduroy with a pink cotton nose and his tail was a piece of grey silk cord. "Happy Christmas Eve," squeaked Charlie to Emily.

"And to you, too!" shouted an excited voice.

A furry monkey called Mickey climbed down from a shelf. He was the colour of caramel with yellow paws and a bendy tail made of brown velvet. He looked around the nursery. "Where's Patch?" he asked.

Patch was a teddy bear and the oldest toy in the nursery. Every year, on Christmas Eve, he told his friends a special story.

Charlie and Emily looked at each other and laughed.

"He's probably still asleep," said Emily. "He's getting old now, you know."

"I'm going to wake him up!" cried Mickey.

Charlie Rat twitched his whiskers. "Do you think Patch will remember our story?" he said. "He's getting quite forgetful, too."

"Of course Patch will remember our story," cried Mickey. "He *has* to remember. It's part of Christmas Eve!"

"I'm sure he will," said Emily, gently. "But we might have to help him a little bit this time."

Patch the teddy bear opened one eye. At first, all he could see were coloured balls, but they didn't look like Christmas decorations. He reached out a threadbare paw and felt around him. He was in some kind of bag and the coloured balls were balls of wool. Very carefully, he stretched out his legs. There were the points of knitting needles on one side and something that felt like a pincushion on the other.

Patch was in the mending bag!

Again!

Poor Patch! It was what happened if you were the oldest toy in the nursery. These days he always needed mending. First it was the patch over his foot. Then it was a patch over his tummy and after that the patch across his back. It wasn't that Patch minded getting old; he didn't care. But he *did* mind if he forgot things.

And the problem was that as Patch got older, he became more and more forgetful. Last year, in the middle of telling the Christmas Eve story about pirates and treasure, he had completely forgotten what came next!

Inside the mending bag, Patch trembled at the memory. If he hadn't caught a glimpse of the gold star on the tree, he would have forgotten all about the chest of gold coins that the pirates had buried in the sand.

And there was no point in telling a

treasure hunt story if there was no treasure.

Patch huddled down in the darkness of the bag. What if the same thing happened this Christmas? "First things first, old bear," he told himself. "Get yourself out of this bag."

"Patch!" It was Emily's voice. "Where are you?"

"In the mending bag," shouted Patch, as loud as he could.

"*Where?*" cried Mickey. "We can't see it anywhere!"

Patch was just about to wriggle out when something dreadful occurred to him.

What if he hadn't been mended? How could he tell a story with his stuffing sticking out?

Patch took a deep breath and ran his paw

carefully over his fur. *Phew!* There was a
square of new cloth just behind his knee!

"Patch!" This time it was Charlie's voice.
"Where *are* you?"

Now that he knew he was mended, Patch
squeezed out of the bag and looked around
him. "I'm stuck on the top shelf of the
cupboard!" he shouted.

"Don't worry!" cried Emily. "We'll get
you out!"

A moment later, the cupboard doors
swung open, and Emily held out her trunk
for Patch to climb down.

"Come on!" cried Charlie. "It's easy!"

But Patch shook his head.
"I can't," he cried.
"I'm afraid of falling!"

"I'll help," said Mickey. "I'm good with heights." So Mickey ran along Emily's trunk, took Patch firmly by the paw and guided him down to the nursery floor.

A minute later, the four friends were sitting around the fire. "Thanks for rescuing me," said Patch. "I could have spent the whole of Christmas trapped in there!"

"No way!" Charlie Rat's black button eyes twinkled. "We'd have found you!"

"Yeah!" cried Mickey. He stood upside down on his paws and waggled his legs in the air. "We'd never miss out on our Christmas Eve story! What is it this time?"

Patch scratched his ears. "I'm not sure," he said. "The problem is every time I remember a story, I forget it two minutes later."

Charlie Rat looked at Emily. "An elephant never forgets," he said. "Can *you* remember a story for Patch?"

"Only Patch can tell our Christmas story," replied Emily. She turned. "Isn't that right, Patch?"

But with all the excitement of getting stuck in the cupboard, Patch had fallen asleep.

Without a word, Mickey and Charlie lifted Patch on to a chair and Emily covered him with a blanket.

Mickey put his head in his paws. "What are we going to do if Patch forgets our story?"

Emily thought hard. "Do you remember last year when he almost forgot about the buried treasure in the pirate story?" she asked.

The others nodded. "I saw him look at the gold star on the tree," Emily went on. "That's what made him remember about the gold coins."

Charlie Rat suddenly caught sight of the patchwork quilt that hung over the back of the sofa. "Why don't we make him something that will help him remember?"

"Like what?" asked Emily.

"How about a patchwork quilt," cried Charlie Rat. "Each patch would remind him of a different story." He grinned. "Like a little piece of red velvet might make you think of a cherry-pie-eating competition!"

"Speak for yourself," said Mickey. "I don't like cherry pie! Besides, I think a patchwork waistcoat would be better." Mickey laughed. "It would cover his patches, too!"

"There's only one problem," said Charlie.

"What?" asked Mickey.

"Where will we find all the bits of cloth we need?"

"Here!" said Emily. She opened the cupboard doors and lifted down the mending bag.

While Patch slept under his blanket, his three friends sat in a circle in front of the fire and sewed scraps of fabric together.

Emily was right. The mending bag was full of snippets from old curtains and blankets and children's clothes. There were patterns with yellow daisies, which could remind Patch of a meadow. One square of cotton had a print of climbing roses like the kind that grew up the walls of country cottages in fairy tales. Another was a piece of shirt covered in racing cars with tiny figures wearing goggles. Patch could make up a brilliant story about them! There was even some shiny silver satin left over from a king's costume in a Christmas play. It could be the silver of the moon or the silver of a space rocket or the glitter of a silver necklace worn by an ancient Egyptian Queen.

Patch would find ideas everywhere!

When the friends finished sewing the patchwork together, Emily drew a pattern on a piece of paper, and Mickey cut out the waistcoat shape with toy scissors. Then Charlie Rat sewed all the pieces together and finished it off with three shiny buttons Emily found in the mending bag.

The waistcoat looked amazing!

Bong! Bong! Bong!

As the grandfather clock at the top of the stairs struck nine, Patch the teddy bear opened one eye. At first he couldn't think how he had got on to a chair and under a blanket. Then he remembered how he had been rescued from the cupboard. "I must have fallen asleep," he said to himself out loud.

He opened both eyes and saw an amazing waistcoat on a stool in front of him.

"What's *that*?" asked Patch.

"It's a present for you," cried Mickey the monkey. "Put it on!"

"A present for me?" said Patch. "What on earth for?"

"To help you make up our story," explained Charlie. He pointed to the patches. "Each one's different, you see."

Patch ran his paws over the silver material from the king's costume. He was already making up a story!

"Thank you!" cried Patch. "It's my best present ever!" He picked up the waistcoat and put it on. It fitted perfectly. "I shall call it my storybook waistcoat."

"What's our story going to be about?" asked Mickey, hopping from foot to foot. "Am I going to be in it?"

"*Everyone's* going to be in it," replied Patch. "Now sit down quietly, Mickey."

"I'm on the chair," cried Charlie, running up the arm and stretching out on the top.

"No, I am!" said Mickey, jumping on to the seat.

"Charlie, Mickey," said Emily, patiently. "The chair's my place. It's always been my place. Why don't you sit down in front of the fire? You'll be warm and cosy there."

"Good idea," cried Mickey. And he jumped off the chair and sat down on the carpet.

When all the friends were settled, Patch took his place in the middle and stared at his waistcoat. He had never known so many stories fill his head!

The fire crackled and a spray of bright sparks floated into the air. "It was our first Christmas Eve in the nursery," said Patch in a low voice. "We pulled back the curtains to look for Father Christmas and saw a huge shiny silver spaceship sitting in the back garden!"

Patch's eyes went round as saucers and his voice dropped to a whisper. "That was the night we flew to the moon!"

The toys shivered with delight. It was so quiet, you could have heard a *whoosh* of stardust tumbling from the sky!

LEO'S GREAT ESCAPE

Holly Webb

"Can we go to bed now, Mum?"

"But Will, it's only four o'clock!" Mum laughed. "And I'm afraid Father Christmas won't come until you're *both* asleep."

Mum and Will both turned to look as a small, sparkly whirlwind blew through the kitchen. Will's little sister Hattie was wearing three tutus, one on top of the other; her favourite pink wellies, and a tiara. She was waving a light-up fairy wand that played "Twinkle, Twinkle, Little Star", but she was singing "Jingle Bells" loudly enough to drown it out. Under her other arm was Susie, the family cat. Susie was looking quite worried. She was used to Hattie treating her like a teddy bear, but Hattie was being a bit madder than usual today.

Will looked back at Mum, his eyes round with panic. "What if she never goes to sleep?"

Mum gave him a hug. "Don't worry. If we can stand the singing for another half an hour, she'll probably fall asleep on the sofa." She glanced down at the table. "What are you making, Will?"

"A Christmas stocking for Leo." Will held up a paper stocking shape.

"Won't he just eat it?" Mum asked gently.

Will rolled his eyes. "Yes, Mum! That's the point! What do hamsters like doing best?"

"Chewing holes in things." Mum frowned, thinking of the school library book that Will had left too close to Leo's cage. She had had to apologize to his teacher for the chewed-up edges, and it had been very embarrassing. Leo was a champion chewer. His cage lived on the window seat in Will's bedroom, and Will's spaceship curtains had a line of little holes along the bottom too. Will said they made the curtains look nicer.

"Exactly," said Will. "And eating. So I'm not going to colour it in, I'm making little holes in it, and I'm going to push sunflower seeds and peanuts into the holes. Those are his absolute favourites."

"Very clever. Have you made a Christmas stocking for me, too?" Mum asked.

Will frowned. "Mum, you're far too old for that."

Mum sighed. "I'll just have a mince pie then. Do you want one?"

"I hate mince pies, they taste all brown." Will shuddered.

"I'll have one." Dad came in, looking a bit stressed. "And I need some coffee." He filled the kettle. Dad had been hiding in the living room with the door shut, wrapping presents. Everyone had been banned, and he'd even put a chair in front of the door after he caught Hattie and Will peering through the keyhole. "We've run out of sticky tape."

Will grinned to himself. That sounded promising! "I'm going to go and give Leo his Christmas stocking," he said, pushing in the last sunflower seed. "I bet he'd like a mince pie, Mum."

Mum shook her head. "Uh-uh. He's fat enough as it is."

Will ran upstairs to his room, opening the door carefully and making sure that Susie and Hattie hadn't followed him. Hattie loved Leo, and always wanted to hold him. But Will worried that she'd accidentally squeeze him too tight – or even worse, that she'd drop him and Leo would disappear somewhere in Will's room.

Susie loved Leo, too – but for all the wrong reasons. Susie thought Leo was a snack on legs, and she seemed to think that Will was just fattening Leo up for her. Perhaps even as a Christmas present.

Will was very careful every time he got the hamster out of his cage. His cousin Josh had a pet mouse called Smartie, and he'd let Smartie out once to explore his model Star Wars spaceship. It had taken three days and trails of sunflower seeds all over Josh's bedroom before Smartie was back in his cage.

"Hey, Leo! Look what I've got for you…" Will opened the cage door, and there was a flurry in the corner of the cage as Leo wiggled himself out of his bedroom. It was stuffed full of bedding, and the door was quite a tight fit for Leo anyway. Eventually he popped out, and pattered over to the door like a little walking snowball. Leo was a white hamster, and very fluffy.

Will put the stocking inside the cage, and Leo looked at it interestedly, sniffing at the peanuts. Then he seized one in his sharp little teeth, and pulled it. It didn't want to come. This time, Leo gave the stocking a determined tug and dragged the whole thing back into bed with him.

Will grinned as Leo's fat white bottom disappeared into his bedroom. He could hear rustling and little satisfied hamster noises. Leo seemed to be enjoying his present. Then he jumped up as Dad yelled from downstairs. It sounded as though something bad had happened – Dad sounded really cross.

Will made for his bedroom door, anxious to see what was going on. He didn't want anything happening to spoil Christmas.

"Hattie, you have to wait until tomorrow! It's not Christmas Day yet!"

Dad was in the hallway, crouching down next to Hattie, who was holding a large present. A large, half-unwrapped present, with the corner of an interesting box poking through...

As he heard Will coming down the stairs, Dad grabbed the present and put it behind his back. "Stop right there!" he told Will. "Hattie went present-hunting, but she opened one of yours. I need to wrap it up again. Right, you two. There's a good film starting in a minute. Just go and watch it, please! And don't come in the living room until I've finished wrapping this up again. Sorry, Will. I'm going to have to hold it together with string…"

Hattie fell asleep watching the film with Susie on her lap, and Will felt pretty sleepy too by the time it was finished. He didn't mind going to bed a bit early – the sooner he was asleep, the sooner it would be Christmas Day.

But as he climbed the stairs to his room, he was suddenly wide awake again.

His bedroom door was open. He *never* left it open!

He thought quickly back to the last time he'd been upstairs. He'd given Leo his stocking. And then he'd heard Dad telling Hattie off and gone down to see what was going on. Will suddenly felt cold – and it was nothing to do with the snow falling outside the landing window.

Had he shut Leo's cage?

Will raced up the last few steps and burst into his room. Then he let out a howl of horror. The cage was wide open, and a few scraps of bedding were scattered on the window seat.

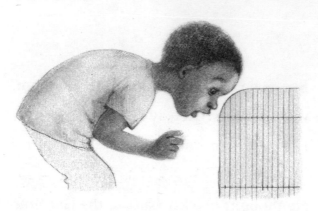

Will checked every corner of the cage just in case, but he knew that Leo wasn't there. He was out. Somewhere in the house – he could be anywhere!

Mum had heard him shout, and hurried into his room. "Oh, Will! He hasn't escaped, has he?"

Will nodded miserably. "And my door was open," he whispered.

"Oh no!" Mum looked horrified. She didn't mind Will having a hamster, but she certainly didn't want one in her bedroom.

Dad put his head round the door. "Did I hear that right? There's a runaway hamster on the loose?"

Will frowned. Dad seemed to be making a joke of it. "What if Susie eats Leo?" he sniffed. He was trying not to cry.

Dad's eyebrows shot up. "I hadn't thought of that! Don't worry, we'll shut Susie in the kitchen. So your bedroom door was open then?"

"Yes!" Will wailed. "I ran downstairs when I heard you telling Hattie off, and I forgot to shut it!"

"Ah!" Dad looked round, as if he hoped Leo would just run past. But there was no little snowball shape trotting along the landing.

But there *was* a cat. Susie had appeared silently, a black shadow creeping up the stairs. Now she was sitting on the top step, looking smug. Her whiskers looked particularly long and shiny – the whiskers of a very well-fed cat.

"Maybe she's eaten Leo already," Will whispered in horror.

"I'm sure she hasn't," Mum said, hugging him. "Don't worry, Will. We'll all look for him. He can't have got far." But Will thought she didn't look too sure.

It had never taken Will so long to get to sleep on Christmas Eve before. He kept sitting up to peer at the special Leo-catcher he'd made out of a tall biscuit tin, a pile of books and an awful lot of sunflower seeds. But there was no hamster in it. They'd looked everywhere. Dad had pulled out all the furniture to check under it, and Hattie had almost capsized the Christmas tree trying to see if Leo had gone to sleep in the tinsel.

Will twitched as he heard a little pattering sound. His heart raced with hope. Were those little hamster feet?

Then he sighed. Just a branch tapping against the window.

Every time he turned over, Will was sure he could see Susie's eyes gleaming in the dark, as she waited to pounce on Leo. Mum had shut Susie in the kitchen as soon as she'd appeared outside Will's door, but Susie was sneaky. Will wouldn't put it past her to escape somehow – if it meant a hamster for Christmas supper.

He felt so guilty. What if he never saw Leo again? Christmas was ruined. He didn't even care what was in that huge parcel any more.

Will lay there, staring at the empty cage on the window seat, and the dark night sky outside. "Please, Father Christmas," he whispered to the stars. "When you come down our chimney, if you see a hamster anywhere…"

Will was deep in a dream of Leo squeaking in horror as a dinosaur pounced on him, when he realized that the squeaking was actually Hattie. She was bouncing on him.

"Wake up! Wake up! I want to open my stocking!"

Will groaned. And then smiled. Christmas morning! Presents!

Then he remembered. His stomach dropped, just like it did in the lift at the shopping centre, and it was as if his heart really was sinking, like they said in books.

"There's lots of things in yours!" Hattie told him excitedly, peering over the end of his bed.

Will nodded. Mum had made him hang up his stocking just before bed last night, even though he said he didn't want to – that all he wanted for Christmas was Leo back. Safe and sound, and all in one piece.

"You've got a chocolate Father Christmas!" Hattie frowned. "I haven't. That's not fair. And you've got a furry thing."

Will didn't really care what was in there, but he didn't want Hattie unpacking his stocking for him, which she was obviously about to do. Besides, he was curious. A furry thing? He wouldn't have thought Father Christmas would bring him a soft toy.

He hauled the stocking on to his lap, and looked inside.

Then he smiled. There was a little white fluffy snowball nestled next to the chocolate figure. Very gently, Will wriggled his hand in, and scooped Leo out of his hiding place. The snowball snuffled sleepily, opened one beady little black eye to stare up at Will – and went back to sleep.

Father Christmas hadn't brought Will a teddy.

He'd brought him back Leo.

THE CURIOUS
LITTLE MOUSE

Malachy Doyle

Esmerelda was a curious mouse, always peeking and peeping and snuffling round the Deep Dark Wood.

One winter's evening, as the rain pitter-pattered on the ground all about her, she heard a roaring. She lifted her head from her cosy little nest by the stream. Then she narrowed her eyes, wiggled her whiskers and wondered.

"Can you hear the roaring?" she asked

her busy brothers, Bob and Billy. "You have to listen really, really hard. I think it's coming from Far Far Away!"

"What roaring? I can't hear a roaring," squeaked Bob, busy with mouse things. "There's far too much to do, Esmerelda — we can't just sit about, *listening*. It's been raining so much we're going to have to find a new place to store our food for the winter!"

"And we need a safe place to hide for when the snow comes!" peeped her oldest brother, Billy. "Anyway, there's no such place as Far Far Away — there's only the wood, silly! Only the Deep Dark Wood!"

Esmerelda tried being whizzy and busy, like Bob and Billy. But she much preferred looking and listening, sitting and thinking and wondering.

So she went to find her friend, Charlie the crow, who lived in the Tallest Tree in the Forest. Charlie always knew everything about everything.

"Can you hear the roaring?" she asked him, over the pitter-patter of the rain.

"Of course I can, Esmerelda," said Charlie, flying down from his nest. "Sometimes it's loud and sometimes it's quiet, but it's always there in the background, even here in the middle of the Deep Dark Wood."

"I knew it!" said Esmerelda. "I knew I wasn't just imagining things! But what is it, Charlie, and why does it roar?"

"It's the Mighty Mighty River," Charlie

told her, "at the edge of the Deep Dark Wood."

"The what? The where?" Esmerelda had never even heard of the Mighty Mighty River. And she'd certainly never been to the edge of the Deep Dark Wood.

"The Mighty Mighty River," Charlie repeated. "It's big and it's wide and it's fast and it roars — especially in winter when there's lots of rain, like today. Do you want to come and see it?"

"I do, I do!" cried Esmerelda.

"Come with me, then," said Charlie. "We'll follow the stream, all the way to the river."

So off Charlie flew, with the little mouse running along behind.

"Oh, oh!" peeped Esmerelda. "I always knew Bob and Billy were wrong. I always knew there must be more than just the Deep Dark Wood!"

The roaring got louder and the stream got bigger, the nearer they came to the Mighty Mighty River.

And when at last they got there, it roared and it sang and it cried and it thundered, and it was so wonderfully wide that a tiny little mouse could hardly even see to the other side.

"It's big, so big!" squeaked Esmerelda, as

loudly as she could over the splashing and the crashing. "And it roars, Charlie! It really truly ROARS!"

"What did I tell you?" said the crow.

Esmerelda scampered up on to a rock at the edge of the river, to watch the water rushing by.

"Don't go too close!" cried Charlie, but it was too late.

SPLASH! A wave broke on the rock, and Esmerelda slipped off, into the Mighty Mighty River.

"Oh, oh!" she squeaked, as she was swept along by the fast-flowing current. "I can't get out, Charlie! Oh, oh – it's freezing!"

Charlie flew down to pluck her from the raging river, but the water beat him back.

"Swim!" he cried. "Swim to the side!"

Esmerelda managed to make her way back to the edge of the river, but she still couldn't get up the steep bank.

"It's too fast!" she gasped. "Too fast and too strong!"

So Charlie went off and found a twig. Then he flew low over the little mouse, who just managed to grab hold of it so Charlie could whisk her to safety.

"Thank you, thank you, thank you!" said Esmerelda, shaking herself dry.

"That's all right," said Charlie. "So now you can see why the Mighty Mighty River's roaring. It's so full of rain!"

"The rain's even heavier now," cried Esmerelda, "and the river's getting bigger all the time. Oh, oh!" she peeped, as the raindrops bounced off her back. "We'd better go and warn Bob and Billy, in case it washes them away, too!"

"Hop on then," said Charlie, "and I'll give you a lift!"

So up she jumped on to his back, and off they flew, through the Deep Dark Wood, all the way home to Esmerelda's busy brothers.

It was a bit scary, flying through the trees, especially with night falling, but the little mouse held on tight.

"Look at the stream, Charlie," she said, gazing down. "It's getting bigger and bigger, too!"

Charlie set her down and then flew back to his nest to check it was still warm and dry.

"I went Far Far Away and I saw it! I saw it!" cried Esmerelda.

"Saw what?" said Bob and Billy, who'd been so busy with mouse things that they hadn't even noticed she'd been gone.

"The Mighty Mighty River, where all the roaring comes from!"

"Don't be silly, sister," said Bob. "There's only the Deep Dark Wood!"

"You're wrong!" cried Esmerelda. "There's the Mighty Mighty River, too! When it rains and rains, like it's raining tonight, it gets bigger and bigger and faster and faster! If you fall in, you might never get out!"

But Bob and Billy wouldn't listen. They just turned away to get on with their whizzy-busy business.

"It's coming! It's coming!" cried Charlie the crow, flying through the darkening trees.

"What is?" said Bob and Billy.

"The Mighty Mighty River!" said Charlie. "It's burst its banks and it's coming this way! Look at the stream!"

The brothers shifted their eyes to the little stream that ran through the wood, and realized that it was much bigger and wider and faster than usual.

They looked for their nest, but they couldn't see it anywhere. All their food was being washed away down the stream! All their hard work had been for nothing!

"Oh, oh!" peeped Bob and Billy.

"Listen!" squeaked Esmerelda.

And the roaring got louder and louder and LOUDER, until even her brothers couldn't help but hear it.

"Quick, everyone!" she cried. "The Mighty Mighty River's coming! We've got to hurry-scurry high, before it washes us all away!"

She started running, and her brothers scampered along behind her, all the way to Charlie's tree, the Tallest Tree in the Forest.

"Up there!" she said, pointing her paw. "That's where we'll be safe from the flood."

"All the way up there?" said Bob, looking up.

"Yes, and I've some food you can share," said Charlie, flying above them.

So up they climbed, higher than they'd ever climbed before, till they got to Charlie's nest at the very top.

Esmerelda's brothers were amazed at all there was to see.

"What a Big Wide World!" sighed Billy, looking down and all around.

"And what a Big Beautiful Sky!" cried Bob, staring at the moon high above him, for the rain had stopped and the sky was clear at last.

"Why didn't you tell us, sister? Why didn't you tell us there was more than just the Deep Dark Wood?"

"I did, I did, but you wouldn't listen!" squeaked Esmerelda.

At the top of the tree, in the shelter of the branches, they had Charlie's warm, dry nest to sleep in, so that's where they spent the night, safe from the rising water.

And every now and again Esmerelda looked out, to see if the Mighty Mighty River was still getting higher. And every time it was!

But in the clear light of morning, when she peered out from the nest, Esmerelda could see that the water was going down again.

And the Mighty Mighty River wasn't rushing quite so fast any more.

"It's safe, it's safe! It's time to go down," she cried.

But they didn't go back to their old home. No, they made themselves a new one, in a cosy little hollow further down the tree, where Esmerelda could keep an eye out for the Mighty Mighty River rising...

Where her busy brother Bob could gaze at the snow, falling out of the Big Beautiful Sky...

And her whizzy brother Billy could stare at the Wonderful Wintery World.

FOOTPRINTS
IN THE SNOW

Narinder Dhami

It was Christmas Eve and Emily was scared. The attic room of the old cottage that she slept in every Christmas was very pretty, with pink walls and a bright pink quilt covering her bed. But still, every noise made her jump, even though she had a night light.

"It'll be all right this time," Emily told herself. "I'm a year older and *much* more sensible. I won't let the twins scare me. I *won't.*"

Beyond the dark windows, enormous, lacy flakes of snow were still drifting silently down. It had started snowing just before Emily and her mum and dad had arrived earlier that afternoon. Every year they spent Christmas with Aunty Sue and Uncle Jack and Emily's cousins Lola and Lily in their cottage in the countryside. The house was in the middle of nowhere on a lonely track. It was surrounded by fields and woods and little else.

"It'll be a white Christmas, Ems," her mum had said, as they unloaded the car. They'd brought lots of food and a big bag of presents to put under the Christmas tree. "Aren't we lucky?"

Suddenly, the door of the attic bedroom

creaked open. Emily's heart began to thump hard as Lola and Lily peeped in.

Emily loved her two cousins, but secretly she was also just a *little* bit nervous around them. No one else knew this, not even Emily's mum and dad.

Lola and Lily were twins and they looked exactly alike. They had long fair hair and large eyes of the brightest blue. Emily thought the twins were beautiful, and she longed to have fair, very straight hair and big blue eyes herself, instead of brown curls and boring brown eyes. Although Lola and Lily were the same age as Emily, they were very brave and nothing ever seemed to worry them. They loved horse-riding and skiing and other sports that seemed quite dangerous to Emily, whose very favourite thing was curling up with a book.

Emily didn't see the twins very often, as they lived so far away. She enjoyed spending Christmas with them, even though she had to leave her little black cat Dizzy behind in the cattery because Mum and Dad said the journey was too long for her. The one and only thing Emily hated was Christmas Eve. Christmas Eve was when it happened. Every year it was *always* the same.

"Are you awake, Ems?" Lola whispered, like she always did.

"Yes," Emily replied, like she always did. Why hadn't she just pretended to be asleep, she wondered. It would save all this trouble.

Lola and Lily padded across the room in their pale blue pyjamas and settled themselves down on the pink quilt.

"Lily's going to start." Lola snuggled down next to Emily. "She *says* it's the scariest story *ever*—"

"It *is*," Lily interrupted. "You won't be able to sleep afterwards."

"Great," Emily said.

Emily couldn't remember exactly when the twins had begun telling ghost stories late on Christmas Eve, after the grown-ups had gone to bed. But it seemed to have been going on for *ever*. She hated ghost stories, but Lola and Lily loved scaring each other to bits. Emily knew the twins had no idea how much she wished the ghost stories would stop. And she simply *couldn't* tell them. Lola and Lily would think she was really silly and boring, and Emily couldn't *bear* that.

"It was a dark, dark night with only a tiny sliver of moon," Lily began.

"You got that from a book," Lola broke in.

Lily ignored her. "Snow was falling," she went on, "and there was no one around.

The little cottage stood at the end of a track, and it was miles from anywhere. The family inside were all asleep. Suddenly…"

Emily felt her heart jump.

"A woman came walking down the track. Her head was bent because of the swirling snow. But do you know what the strangest thing of all was?"

"No," Emily whispered.

"*She left no footprints in the snow behind her,*" Lily said softly.

Emily's tummy lurched.

"Inside the cottage the dog woke up. He could smell something dangerous coming. He lifted his head and howled in terror."

Emily shivered.

"The cottage door was locked, but

slowly it began to swing open. And then the dog heard a noise — a thin, terrible, haunting wail."

WAAAAAAAAHHH!

"What was that?" Emily gasped. Lily hadn't made that noise. The thin, terrible, haunting wail had come from outside the cottage.

WAAAAAAAAHHH!

"There it is again!" Lola looked just as terrified as Emily. "Go and look out of the window, Lily."

"No way!" Lily shook her head, her eyes wide with fear. "I'll wake Mum and Dad."

She ran out of the room and Lola followed.

"Don't leave me!" Emily called, but they

didn't hear her. Shaking all over, Emily pulled the duvet over her head. But still she heard the wailing, although it was muffled this time.

WAAAAAAAAHHH!

Suddenly, Emily frowned. The noise reminded her of Dizzy, when the little cat had hurt her paw once. Throwing back the duvet, she jumped out of bed and ran down the twisty wooden stairs to the narrow hallway.

Emily opened the front door and the snow blew right in, making her gasp. But there on the step was a tiny ginger furball of a kitten. He was dusted with snowflakes and he stared up at Emily with big, frightened eyes.

"Where have *you* come from?" Emily asked. She could see that the kitten was still very little, maybe only a month old. Carefully she picked him up and gave him a warming cuddle. He mewed happily, snuffling at Emily's neck. But then, in the light from the hallway, Emily spotted a dark shape in the garden. It was a black and white cat. She was struggling through the deep snow away from the house towards the gate.

"Here, puss!" Emily called. She guessed that this was the mother cat. Had she left her kitten on the doorstep, looking for a safe place on this snowy night?

The cat turned her head. *WAAAAAHHH!* she wailed. It was the same sound Emily and the twins had heard earlier. *It's a desperate cry for help,* Emily thought. She could see that the cat was very thin and looked tired out. It was probably a stray.

Emily called out to the cat again, but the cat continued on her way. She slipped out of the gate and went off down the track.

Where is she going? Emily wondered anxiously. Could she have *more* kittens somewhere that needed shelter? Soon she would be swallowed up by the darkness and the snow, out of Emily's sight...

Emily could hear noises upstairs, but she didn't have time to wait for the grown-ups. She put the ginger kitten safely in the kitchen, closing the door behind her. Then she grabbed her mum's coat, which was closest, put on her hat and shoved her bare feet into her wellies. Uncle Jack's torch was on the hall table so she took that, too.

She went outside, leaving the front door slightly open so that she could slip back into the house again. She hoped no one would realize she'd gone out, but if they did, they'd be able to follow her footprints and come after her. Her mum and dad would be very angry, Emily knew, but she couldn't let the black and white cat go alone into the cold, snowy night. What if she was right, and there *were* more kittens out there?

She hurried down the track by the light of the torch. "Where are you, puss?"

she called. The cat had vanished. But Emily could see a trail of paw prints in the snow. She followed the trail through a gap in the hedgerow and into a field.

The snow was stopping now, but the icy wind was beginning to swirl it around, blowing it into deep, white drifts. Snowflakes covered Emily's hat, and her mum's coat was soon soaked. But she kept going.

The paw prints led Emily across another field, and then another. Soon she was completely lost. But at last she caught sight of the cat ahead of her. She had stopped on the edge of a ditch and was mewing loudly.

Emily pointed her torch down towards the ditch and saw two more kittens – one tabby, and one black and white like its mother. They were huddled together, looking cold and miserable.

The cat jumped down into the ditch, and picked up the black and white kitten in her mouth. Emily was sure now that the cat had been desperate to find a safe place for her babies, and that was what had brought her to the cottage.

"I'll carry the other kitten," Emily said,

stroking the cat's back. It was so thin, she could feel her knobbly backbone. "And we'll all go back to the cottage together."

Carefully, she scooped up the tabby kitten and tucked her safely inside her mum's coat, before zipping it up. She was small and thin, and wriggled a little, but as she warmed up, she began to purr.

"Let's go," Emily said to the cat. She shone the torch on the snow, searching for her footprints so she could find her way home. But there were none to be seen. With a sinking heart, Emily realized that the drifting snow had completely covered her trail.

Emily tried not to panic. She looked around trying to spot the cottage, but it was hopeless. She couldn't see any lights anywhere. If her parents had noticed that she was missing by now, *they* wouldn't be able to follow her footsteps to find her, either.

Still carrying her kitten, the mother cat padded away across the field again. She looked back to check that Emily was following with the other one.

"It's up to you, now," Emily told her.

There was nothing else Emily could do. She had to trust the mother cat to find her way back to the place where she'd left her ginger kitten. Emily stumbled after her. Her feet were freezing and she was wet through. But she could feel the warmth of the tabby kitten against her chest and hear her soft purring.

All of a sudden – there was the cottage! Light was blazing from every window and the front door stood open. Emily's mum and dad and Uncle Jack were out in the front garden. As they saw Emily and the cat coming, they all ran down the track towards them through the deep snow. Emily had never seen her mum run so fast. Aunty Sue, Lily and Lola were peering out of the front door, Lily holding the ginger kitten.

"Emily, where have you been?" her mum cried out with relief. "We were so worried. We've only just realized you were missing!"

"Mind the kitten!" Emily whispered, as first her mum, and then her dad, hugged her tightly. "I left the front door open so that you'd know I went out. Didn't you see?"

Uncle Jack shook his head. "The wind must have blown it shut," he said. "The twins found the ginger kitten, and we couldn't *think* how it had got into the kitchen!"

"And then your mum noticed that her coat and your wellies weren't there, so we guessed you'd gone out," Dad added, keeping his arm around Emily's shoulders. "But we didn't know which way you'd gone because the drifting snow had covered your footprints." He bent down to pat the mother cat, then looked up. "Come inside, all of you, and get warm."

A little later, they all sat in front of the blazing log fire, snuggled up in blankets and sipping hot chocolate. It was officially Christmas now, Emily thought happily, because it was well after midnight. The Christmas tree in the window was lit up, and Emily had fed the cat, who in turn had fed her kittens. Now they were asleep, curled up on the rug together in one large furry ball.

"What will happen to them, Mum?" Emily asked, as she sipped her mug of hot chocolate. She stared hopefully at her parents.

Mum smiled. "Maybe Dizzy would like a couple of friends," she suggested. "We could keep two of the kittens."

"Oh, yes, please!" Emily gasped, her face lighting up even more brightly than the

Christmas tree. "But what about the mother cat and the other kitten?"

"Mum and Dad have said *we* can keep the cat," Lily piped up.

"And one of the kittens, too," Lola added.

Emily's smile grew wider. Now all the kittens and the mother cat would have good homes. "But it's so difficult to choose..." She stared down at the cat and her babies sleeping peacefully. "The tabby and the black and white kitten are quiet and gentle, like Dizzy, so I think they'd like each other. Would you like the ginger kitten?" she asked Lola and Lily. The ginger kitten was perfect for the twins. He was very bold and cheeky and confident. He'd already tried to climb up the Christmas tree twice.

The twins looked thrilled.

"Yes, please!" said Lily. "We thought we'd call the mother cat Santa and the kitten Claws."

"And I'll call the black and white kitten Jingle," Emily decided. "The tabby can be Belle."

"Santa, Claws, Jingle and Belle." Aunty Sue smiled. "What lovely, Christmassy names!"

"You were really brave, Emily," Lola said, as their parents chatted over their hot chocolate. "You went downstairs to see what was making that noise all on your own."

"You went out into the dark, too, and you weren't scared one bit," Lily added.

"Oh, I *was*," Emily replied. "I was *very* scared."

But she was very sure now that Christmas Eve would never, ever be so scary again.

Have you read…